# Riddles Teasers for Kids Ages 10-12

## Riddles and Jokes Trick Questions for Kids

Copyright: Published in the United States by Melissa Smith/
© 2019 Melissa Smith All right reserved.

All rights reserved. No part of this publication may be reproduced, stored in retrieval system, copied in any form or by any means, electronic, mechanical, photocopying, recording or otherwise transmitted without written permission from the publisher. Please do not participate in or encourage piracy of this material in any way. You must not circulate this book in any format. Melissa Smith does not control or direct users' actions and is not responsible for the information or content shared, harm and/or actions of the book readers.

In accordance with the U.S. Copyright Act of 1976, the scanning, uploading and electronic sharing of any part of this book without the permission of the publisher constitute unlawful piracy and theft of the author's intellectual property. If you would like to use material from the book (other than just simply for reviewing the book), prior permission must be obtained by contacting the author at thebookhivenet@gmail.com
Thank you for your support of the author's rights.

**WWW.THEBOOKHIVE.NET**
**VISIT PAGE: FACEBOOK.COM/THEBOOKHIVEDOTNET**

FOLLOW ME: AMAZON.COM/AUTHOR/MELISSAS

# Introduction

This is a fun riddle book that contains a lot of riddles and tricky brain teasers of easy to hard difficulty. Make children think and stretch their minds. It is a perfect activity book for kids who like problem-solving.

Great book of Riddles and Brain Teasers for Kids.
These activities can be shared with the whole family. With this book, you will keep your kids and their friends busy and entertained for hours! It's also perfect for families, parties or even youth group events!

This book is one of the series Riddles,
Puzzles, Trick Questions
This is kid's books that design to challenge children to think laterally and more creatively. This book offers an experience that you and your family will absolutely enjoy.

## CHECK OTHER BOOKS IN SERIES

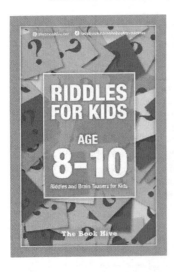 

**WWW.THEBOOKHIVE.NET**
**VISIT PAGE: FACEBOOK.COM/THEBOOKHIVEDOTNET**
FOLLOW ME: AMAZON.COM/AUTHOR/MELISSAS

What kind of makeup is used for finger tips?

_____

What do you think is the reason of the woman
why she throws a bucket of water out the window?

_____

What is the best way to jump out of
the step ladder without being hurt?

_____

What do you call the red stuff
between elephant's toes?

_____

What do you think is the reason of the teenager
why he puts his clock in the oven?

_____

What is the second L in LOL?

_____

1

What have strong affection for belly buttons?

_____

What is the best way to cure hair dandruff?

_____

What is it that no men want,
but no men want to lose?

_____

What specific question can never
get an answer "YES" anymore?

_____

What will be the response of the student
in this classroom discussion?
The teacher we're going to talk
about the tenses.
Teacher: Now, if I say "I am beautiful,"
which tense is it?

_____

What is it that in life, it must bare,
and bloodline must share?

_____

What is always in front of you,
but you will never see?
1) Present    2) Past    3) Future


What would be the relationship they have to each
other if the two teachers teach at the same school,
one is the father of the other's son?

_____


What would be an old tan
broken down house wear outside?

_____


Which season have a shorter day,
in winter or in summer?

_____


What is a comical rabbit?

_____


What can be simple or can be complex,
and can be found in this riddle,
or in everyday life,
and can also be shapes or even colors?

_____

What can be cracked,
made, told and played?

_____

Where is the best place to
send a horse when it is sick?

_____

What can alter the strengths of a king and
leave puzzled the greatest of philosophers?

_____

What kind of game
do cows play at parties and events?

_____

What is the reason of the man
why he puts the clock in the safe?

_____

What  is it that goes up
and never comes down
no matter how hard you wish,
as it gets higher,
more wrinkles crawl on to the face?

_____

Who owned by every man,
though length differs,
their wives uses it after getting married?

_____

What is this letter of the alphabet
that is always waiting in order?

_____

What do
brothers and sisters have none
but that man's father is the father's son?

_____

Who has no small athletic feat,
has to stay nimble on his feet,
to fight and his opponents beat,
and taste sweet victory, not grim defeat?

_____

What is the reason of the man in throwing his
watch out of the window?

_____

What is it that always around you
but often forgotten,
pure and clean most time,
but occasionally rotten?

_____

What is it that can be long or short,
can be grown or bought,
and can be painted or left bare,
and the tip can be round or square?

_____

What specific state in the United States
is high in the middle and round at the ends?

_____

What is the reason of the woman
why she wear a helmet at the dinner table?

_____

Who is that someone you don't know?

_____

What is the reason of the teenager
why she puts sugar under her pillow?

_____

What is the only place today before yesterday?

_____

What is taken from me
and then locked up in  a wooden case,
and never released
but used by students everyday?

_____


When can we say that a man be six feet tall
and be short at the same time?

_____


What is this outcome, already written,
fight it and you'll be smitten,
by it you may be blessed,
or put up to the test,
and take you places you'd have never guessed?

_____


What did one potato chip say to the other?

_____


What is the best exercise for losing weight?

_____


What is it that can never be stolen from you,
owned by everyone,
and some have more, some have less?

_____

What is it that dance on one feet
and knows only one shape,
someone with same name as me
and is very good directions?

_____

What occurs once in a minute, twice in
a moment, and not once in a hundred years?

_____

Why is it that sailors couldn't play cards?

_____

What do you call a Spaniard
who can't find his car?

_____

What is it that whoever made it don't want it,
whoever bought it, don't need it,
and whoever use it, don't know it?

_____

Who is a mother from a family of eight,
spins around all day despite my weight,
had a ninth sibling before founding out its fake?
1) Earth    2) Sun    3) Comets


What do you get if you cross a baby
with a U.F.O.?

_____


What is the best thing that you should do
if a bull charges you?

_____


What are these seven brothers, five work all day,
the other two, just play or pray?

_____


What's the best thing to take when
you're run over by a vehicle?

_____


What is when you take away the whole from it,
there is always some left?

_____


**9**

What word becomes longer
when the third letter is removed?

_____

What was awarded
to the inventor of door knockers
given at the People's Choice Award?

_____

What did the outlaw get
when he stole a calendar?

_____

Can you name this riddle?
I am a word,
I sometimes enter with a gong.
All in order from A to Z,
I start with the letter B.

_____

What is it that has a fork and mouth,
but cannot eat?

_____

What is it that enjoyed by some,
despised by others,
some take it for granted,
some treasure it like a gift,
and it last forever, unless you break it first?

_____

Who is a king
who's good at measuring stuff?

——————————

What letters do Tuesday, Thursday,
Friday and Saturday have in common?

————————————————————

What is the reason
why didn't the hot dog star in the movies?

————————————————————

What is it that has many shapes, many sizes,
can't be seen, only felt, can bring pain,
can bring joy, bring laughter, bring happiness,
and can tear the mightiest from their thrones,
and those who have it are rich?

——————————

What do tigers have
that no other animals have?

————————————

What is it that my first half means container,
not a lot of people understand the language?

——————————

What walks on 4 legs in the morning,
2 legs  in the afternoon
and 3 legs at night?

_____


What do you think is the reason
why number six is afraid ?

_____


Can you name this riddle?
Deep, deep, it goes,
spreading out as they go,
never needing any air,
they are sometimes as fine as hair.

_____


What has ten letters and starts with gas?

_____


What do you think
is longest word in the dictionary?

_____


Who has a feathers that help him fly,
with head and body but not alive.
very skinny and a fixed length,
how far it goes depends on?

_____

**What is free at the first time and second time,
but the third time is going to cost you money?**

1) Teeth     2) Shoulder     3) Hair

**What is this word that everybody
always says wrong?**

_____

**What is useful tool for who in darkness dwell,
within you, corrupting like a deadly spell?**

_____

**What is the object that is
long and filled with seamen?**

_____

**What kind of running means walking?**

_____

**What is this certain thing that
go in dry and come out wet,
and the longer it stays in,
the stronger the surroundings get?**

_____

What would you have that you want to share,
but once you share it, you won't have it?

_____


How would you spell mousetrap?

_____


What is this natural state, that sought by all,
go with it and you shall fall,
you do it when you spend,
and you use it when you eat to no end?

_____


Can you guess this riddle?
It's first is ocean but not in sea.
It's second in milk but not in me.
It's third is in three but not in throw.
It's fourth in vow but not in crow.
Fifth is in eight but not in night.
And last is in wrong and also right.
It's whole is praise for thoughts or men;
Or women, too, or tongue or pen.

_____


Can you name five things that contain milk?

_____


What is this thing that we all need
yet we give it away everyday?

_____

What will be the ending
of all that has begun?

_____


What is special day for cooking
bacon and eggs?

_____


What object has sides,
that are firmly laced,
yet nothing is within,
you'll think the head is strange indeed,
being nothing else but skin?

_____


What nukes food at the touch of a button?
1) Microwave    2) Rice Cooker    3) Stove


When will be the time
that the money will rain?

_____


What can't go left and can't go right,
and forever stuck in a building
over three stories high?

_____

What is that you lose,
that may cause people to lose you too?

_____


What do you think is the letter of the alphabet
that has got lots of water?

_____


What is made of ten but two we make,
when assembled others quake,
five apart and we are weak,
five together havoc wreak?

_____


What is beautiful as the setting sun,
as delicate as the morning dew;
an angel's dusting from the stars,
that can turn the Earth into a frosted moon?
1) Snow    2) Rain    3) View


What is this  certain thing that grows bigger
the more you take from it?

_____


What instrument
is capable of making numerous sound
but cannot be touched or seen?

_____

Who is this that cloud is her mother,
and wind is her father?

_____


What do you call a noisy group of people?

_____


Do you know this object
that must be in pair,
but usually alone you see,
for a monster always eats it?

_____


What is this tool of thief, toy of queen,
always used to be unseen,
sign of joy, sign of sorrow,
giving all likeness borrowed?

_____


Who are the relatives
that are dependent on you?

_____


What is black, white, and can be read all over?

_____

**What is a mountain at night,
and meadow at day?**
1) Bed     2) Moon     3) Star


**What do you think are the
two strongest days of the week?**

_____


**What part of the bird, that is not in the sky,
which can swim in the ocean
and always stays dry?**

_____


**What is rather large and usually majestic,
every hue of the rainbow,
and can eat you, may hit you,
and you only wish you could see it?**

_____


**Who is the football player
wears the biggest helmet?**

_____


**What runs around the streets all day,
under the bed or by the door,
sits at night, never alone.
and the tongue hangs out,
waiting to be fed during the day?**

_____

What is a necessity to some,
a treasure to many,
best enjoyed among pleasant company,
some like me hot, some like me cold
some prefer mild and some like me bold?

_____

What do you think is the reason,
why do birds fly south for the winter?

_____

What has wings, but can not fly,
it is enclosed, but can outside also lie,
can open itself up, or close itself away,
and it is the place of kings and queens,
and it is a place where in we can stand
which can lead us to different lands?

_____

What is sharp slim blade, that cuts the wind?

_____

What kind of driver
never commits a traffic offense?

_____

What is it that you cannot keep
until you have given it?

_____

What can go from house to house,
a messenger small and tight,
weather it rains or snows,
may sleep outside at night?

_____


What do you think is the reason of the student
to take a ladder to school?

_____


Can you guess this riddle?
A time when it is green.
A time when it is brown.
But both of these times, cause me to frown.
But just in between, for a very short while.
It is perfect and yellow.
And cause me to smile.

_____


What is a foot long
and can be used in pair by our feet?

_____


What are the three letters of the alphabet
do all the work?

_____


What will hold two people together
but touch only one?

_____

What is it that you turn over
after you have travelled far?

_____

What can you see all over the house?

_____

What house where you are brought,
if they find you or get caught.
if you cross the government,
this is where you will be sent?

_____

What is this object that acts as
an addition to the dental benefits,
having one of these hanging out of your
mouth will make you look like a wise guy?

_____

What do you call a person
who doesn't have all his fingers on one hand?

_____

What would break you but continued to work,
touch you and maybe stays with you forever?

_____

What is this object that won't break
if you throw it off
from the highest building
but will break if you place it in the ocean?

_____

What is it that no man ever yet did see,
which never was, but always will be?

_____

What is it that never rest, never still,
moving silently from hill to hill,
it does not walk or run,
all is cool where it is not?
1) Sunshine    2) Sunset    3) Rain

What is it that the first is an insect,
second is a border,
and the whole puts the face
in a tuneful disorder?

_____

What is the best way to make a lemon drop?

_____

What hide in a dark tunnel
awaiting for the time,
and can only be released by pulling back,
once released, may do unstoppable damage?

_____

What is it that Physicists have built devices
to move very fast and the last seven letters
can be commonly found in newspapers,
magazines and journals?

_____

What do you think is the part of London that
can be found in France?

_____

What stage in your life
when you simultaneously know everything
and nothing at an instance?

_____

What do you think is the reason of a
firefighter in wearing red suspenders?

_____

What exists when you are here,
where you never were, it can never be?

_____

What kind of ship can be made
to ride the greatest waves,
not built by objects
but built by heart and mind?

_____


What do you think
is the most self-centered letter
of the alphabet?

_____


What is it that you roll or you buy,
people say you shouldn't try it,
because you may get a stroke,
from inhaling all that smoke?

_____


What kind of group who manages
the winged engines of war?

_____


What do you think
is a teacher's favorite nation?

_____


What was not born but here,
have no name, but given many,
and was made by science and life?

_____

What belongs to everyone,
sometimes make you happy,
sometimes make you sad
and will never end until the day you do?

_____

What do you call a witch at the beach?

_____

What is this horrid monster
that hides from the day,
with   many legs and many eyes,
with silver chains it catches prey,
and eats it all before it dies,
yet in every cottage does it stay,
and every castle beneath the sky?

_____

What would you feel
if you are having a bad day
if 12 peers deem you to be this?

_____

What is a joyful father?

_____

What can generate fear and some say
it comes out of your ears,
it is quite as a mouse,
but not welcomed in the house?

_____

What drifts forever with the current
and flows to your everyday life,
makes living easy,
but good at killing people too?
**1**) Gun    2) Electricity    3) Water

How much dirt can we have in a hole exactly
one foot deep and one foot wide?

_____

What is it that is long and thin
and make things right,
and will repair your mistakes
but watch the bite?

_____

What kind of vehicle
can get you there in eco style,
pushed by your legs mile after mile?
1) Bicycle    2) Tricycle    3) Car

What is the reason
why baseball stadiums so cool?

_____

What is it that have 24 keys
but cannot open any locks
sometimes loud, sometimes soft?

_____

Who can swim but never get wet,
can run but never get tired,
and follows you everywhere
but never say a word?

_____

How many people are buried in that cemetery?

_____

What is this object that
although a human shape it wear,
Mother, it never had;
and though no sense nor life it share,
in finest silks it clad,
by every miss it valued much,
beloved and highly prized,
cruel fate is such
by boys it is often despised?

_____

What is it that may only be given,
not taken or bought,
what the sinner desires,
but the saint does not?

_____

What do you call a dog with no legs?

_____

What is in the past, never in the future,
don't exist, but have existed?
saw what you saw,
this is what I will ever see?

_____

What is it that have been argued
on they colour,
without it you'll die,
so many attempts on your life use it,
so make sure you have
many of my "White" friends?

_____

What can you serve, but never eat?

_____

What is small, but, when entire,
of force to set a town on fire,
let but one letter disappear,
then can hold a herd of deer,
take one more off, and then you'll find it
once contained all human kind?

_____

What can be clear like water,
but it burns like fire?

_____

Why do egg goes into the jungle?

_____

What is easy to waste and unstoppable?

_____

28

What is one small little piece of paper,
yet sometimes hold lots of value,
all you need to get in to big events,
but will cost you,
and an important part of travel,
and if lost, you're not coming?

_____

What is it that has two heads, four eyes,
six legs and a tail?

_____

What is it that every team needs one of these
before hitting the field,
and get pumped?

_____

Who is this person that
prefers to travel on vines
and pal around with gorillas?

_____

What gets dirty by washing?

_____

What will bring things together,
without me everything you see
would be a total mass or debris everywhere?

_____

What may seems real but it always turns out,
never there in the first place,
and you only see during a certain resting stage?

_____

What is something that frogs do very well
and can be the sound of a ringing bell?

_____

What is more rare today than long ago,
and written below,
there's a salutation from friends?

_____

Can a kangaroo jump higher
than the Empire State Building?

_____

What is it that you get embarrassed
when you stand on it,
when everybody is watching,
women don't like to talk about
the number they see on it
and everyone stands on it
when nobody is around?

_____

Who have married many women
but has never been married?

_____

What was it that
I saw a nutcracker up in a tree?

_____

If 5 men catch 5 fishes in 5 minutes,
how long will it take one man
to catch a fish?

_____

What letter is always trying to find reasons?

_____

What are three simple words,
everyone wants to hear,
three simple words,
but life changing?

_____

31

What is it that many people own a copy of it,
and without it, the world would fall?

_____

How many bumpers were
actually touching each other,
if there were five automobiles
that were lined up bumper to bumper?

_____

What is it that chopped its feet
and we drink its blood?

_____

What is it that twists and turns,
but has no curves,
twist it to fix it, turn it to ruin it?

_____

What would be the best way to win a race?

_____

What is a small paradise
surrounded by dryness and heat?

_____

What would encourage people
to run home and steal?

_____


What part of your body disappears
when you stand up?

_____


What is it that we give a toss, and it's ready,
but not until it's dressed?

_____


What is it that used to bat with,
yet never get a hit,
near a ball, yet it is never thrown?

_____


What is the reason
why the skeleton didn't go to the dance?

_____


What is a daily ritual involving
using a metal tool on the body?

_____

Who do you think have a strong affection
for belly buttons?

_____

What do you call a bear without an "ear"?

_____

What is it in the forest,
this blends in just right,
but every December it is covered with lights?

_____

What is it that the more holes you cover
the lower it goes?

_____

What did the fish say when he hit the wall?

_____

What is the sound made
by felines when petted?

_____

What noise do cats and deflation tires make?

_____

How far do you have to count before
using the letter A in spelling a number?

_____

What kinds of men are always above board?

_____

What is it that if you feed it, it will live,
if you give it water, it will die?
1) Fire    2) Earthquake    3) Typhoon

What is  longer than a decade
and shorter than a millennium?

_____

What is it that you need thousands,
to create a digital image?

_____


What is the reason why birds fly
to south in the winter?

_____


What is whole but incomplete,
have no eyes, yet can see,
and the largest part is one fourth
of what once was?

_____


What binds couple yet touches only one?
**1)** Ring    2) Necklace    3) Earrings


What do you think is the difference
between a lion with toothache and a wet day?

_____


Where can we still find the Titanic?

_____

What do teenage girls are pros at creating
and can be learned in classes?

_____

What can makes a cow fly?

_____

What becomes too young the longer it exists?

_____

What is a life or death skill for gunfighters?

_____

What type of animal
that hangs out in the mist?
1) Gorilla    2) Dog    3) Cat

What is used when you jump off
a bridge for fun?

_____

What continent do you see when you
look in the mirror in the morning?

_____

What is a long snake that smokes?

_____

What kind of gemstone
that a certain wizard resided in a city made?

_____

What part of your body
can you hold in your left hand,
but not in your right hand?

_____

What specific object mirrors your actions?

_____

**Who will direct you from outer space?**
1) Compass    2) GPS    3) Ruler


**How many bricks does it take
to finish a house?**

_____


**What can you hold in the hand
when going out?**

_____


**When is 1500 plus 20 and 1600
minus 40 the same thing?**

_____


**What do you think is the longest word?**

_____


**What do you call a digital white-out?**

_____

What can be heard in a court
and carried with you?

_____

Which letter is not me?

\_\_\_\_\_

What is it that have many ears,
this may be true,
but no matter how you shout,
it will never hear you?

_____

What are these tiny creatures
that have a special relationship with flowers?

_____

What has a neck, but no head?

_____

What is the score in end zones?

_____

What do you call a skirts for men?

_____

What state is very expensive to live?

_____

What has 8 arms and lots of ink
but can't write a word?

_____

What has feet and legs and nothing else?

_____

How many sheep do we need
to make one wool sweater?

_____

What help engines spin and pants stay up?

_____

What is a path between high natural masses,
remove the first letter to get a path
between man-made masses?

_____

What happens to a refrigerator
when you pull its plug?

_____

Which do you light up first
and you only have 1 match,
and if there are 3 stoves:
a glass stove, a brick stove, and a wood stove?

_____

What kind of beer yet kids can drink me
and not get drunk?

_____

What kind of bushes do rabbits in
California sit under when it rains?

_____

What hatch without food?

_____

What is that sweet when young,
when middle aged, makes you gay,
and when old, valued more than ever?
1) Wine     2) Coffee     3) Soda


What is an animal that eats a paper
or can be the cloak of a Roman man?

_____


What kind of vegetable
is the king of rock and roll?

_____


What kind of vegetable do people
look forward to getting every month?

_____


What do you think is the difference
between a jeweler and a jailor?

_____


What is perfect with or without a head,
perfect with or without a tail,
and perfect with either, neither or both?

_____


**43**

What cut through evil
like a double edged sword,
and chaos flees at its approach,
balance single-handedly upraise,
through battles fought with heart and mind,
instead of with its gaze?

_____

When do we say that it's bad luck
to have a black cat following you?

_____

What can you throw but not catch?

_____

What is the sweetest and most romantic fruit?

_____

Which side would the egg roll off
if a rooster laid an egg on top of a
pointed-roof henhouse?

_____

What can be repeated
but rarely in the same way,
and can't be changed but can be rewritten,
can be passed down,
but should not be forgotten?

_____

What is it that hot and cold,
the parent of numbers that cannot be told,
a gift beyond measure, a matter of course,
and given with pleasure when taken by force?

_____

What produces a flower but it is not its fruit,
and it produces branches which are its fruit?

_____

What object is never used
unless it's in a tight place?

_____

During the class discussion,
the teacher ask the students:
Teacher -First came the Ice Age,
then - the Stone Age. What came next?

_____

What kind of soda you must not drink?

_____

What is a dragons tooth in a mortals hand,
that kills and divides the land?

_____

What do you think is the most colorful
state of U.S.A.?

_____

What vegetable can you find
all sorts of animals?

_____

What is a pal of the peanut
and loves to sing along and play music?

_____

How should you dress on a cold day?

_____

What is it that in your fire,
you hear screaming, creaking and whining,
yet dead  before you lay it in your heart?

_____

What soar without wings, see without eyes,
travelled the universe to and from
and conquered the world,
yet  never been anywhere but home?

_____


What can be measured,
even without length, width, or thickness?

_____


What kind of food loves to yell and shout?

_____


What get chewed, but should not be
swallowed or eaten
and always get thrown away?

_____


Why do you think roosters are considered
the neatest birds?

_____


What can be swallowed,
but can also swallows you?

_____

What can fly away if you set it loose
and never so cursed as when it goes astray?

_____

What do you think the cannibal would get
if he was late for a dinner?

_____

Who is the father of all fruits?

_____

What kind of room can you eat?

_____

What do you call an objects that
asks no questions
but receives a lot of answers?

_____

What can you see if you stop and look,
and if you try to touch, you cannot feel,
it also cannot move, but as you near to it,
it will moves away from you?

_____

What is it that the first is high,
second is damp,
whole a tie, a writer's camp?

_____


What kind of nail should you never hit
with a hammer?

_____


What do you call the kind of dessert
that is the best chef?

_____


What kind of food do you eat
when you take a break at school?

_____


What direction will the smoke blows
if an electric train travels ninety miles
an hour in a westerly direction
and the wind is blowing from the north?


What is sometimes white,
but most often black,
it takes you there,
but never bring you back?

_____

What have leaves on fruit,
and fruit is on the leaves?
1) Pineapple    2) Apple    3) Mango


What is the capital of "England"?
_____


What is this place that sounds so cool
and people all over the world come again
and again to see it,
most people spend years with but you can't
be too old or young to come unless you decide
to make the part of your career,
and this place will makes you
smarter and wealthier too?
1) School    2) Hospital    3) Canteen


What did the janitor say to another janitor
when they got arrested for stealing diapers?
_____


During the class discussion, the teacher says:
"John, name two pronouns."
What do you think
would be the response of John?
_____


What is this fruit that when you squeeze
will cry tears as red as flesh,
but the heart is made of stone?
_____

What is it that the first is a heir,
second's a snare,
whole is the offspring of fancy,
which sent out of play,
upon Valentine's day as a token of love?

_____


Who do you think tells chicken jokes?

_____


Who is a rebel, impulsive, typical, awkward,
annoying, sometimes bitter
and sometimes sweet?

_____


Where does a student go
to scope out a new school?

_____


What is it that this moment,
everyone in the world
is doing the same thing?

_____


What can you read in both ways,
one way it's a number, reversed a snare?

_____

What do keepers feed with colored balls,
with sticks they store on the den walls,
sometimes stores in the pouch,
sometimes deep in the belly?

_____

What is it that he more you take,
the more you leave behind?

_____

Why is it that teenagers make
great parole officers?

_____

What do you call a thumb but no fingers
and is not living?

_____

What do you call a vehicle
that has four wheels and flies?

_____

What is that object that
has weight in the belly, trees on the back,
nails in the ribs and feet do lack?
1) Boat    2) Plane   3) Bicycle

What is it that starts in little but end in full,
and you'll find it in half and complete?

_____

What do you think is the reason
why the little drops of ink were crying?

_____

What is a simple for a few people,
but hard for them to hear,
live inside of secrets,
and bring people's worst fears?

_____

What kind of table has no legs?

_____

What do you call a deer without eyes?

_____

What causes involuntary movements
in your vehicle?

_____

Who is this boy that although sounds like
he works on a transportation device,
he actually works in a restaurant?

_____


What do you call a beautiful cat?

_____


What is the electronic version of junk mail
or a salty meat in a can?

_____


What is this way to cross a water,
that you won't touch the water above
and truth to say, it neither swim nor move?

_____


What do you call
an uncontrollable boy or girl?

_____


What is a mini solar powered computer?

_____

What do you call a lunch money thief?

_____

What do you call an unusual seat?

_____

What snacks that is being served
at a robot party?

_____

What is this object that if you eat,
the sender will also eat you?

_____

How come none of them wet
if six students and two teachers
were under just one umbrella?

_____

What is an activity involving pins
lying in the air?

_____

What action can be done on mosquito bites?

_____

What is this that the first is equality,
second is inferiority
and the whole is superiority?

_____

What is one of the few vegetables that is
routinely consumed with marshmallows?

_____

A cowgirl had twelve cows.
All but nine died.
How many cows did she have left?
1) Nine    2) Twelve    3) One

What can destroy your home from inside out.

_____

What kind of car that when you are inside,
you will be encouraged to slam other cars?

_____

What do you call an angry boy?

_____

What can you a lot of iron without getting sick?

_____

What do you think the angry electron would
say when it was repelled?

_____

What do you call a bashful insect?

_____

What expelled from you orally with a sound?

_____

What is the best thing that can happen
after a stick hits a ball?

_____

If you count twenty cows on your
right going into the farm,
and twenty cows on your left coming home,
how many cows have you counted in all?

_____

What element is a girl's future best friend?

_____

What should you do with a dead chemist?

_____

Which do you think is better:
"The house burned down"
or "The house burned up"?

_____

What transfers oxygen
from the atmosphere to your blood?

_____

Who would applaud if you perform well?

_____

What is a god, a planet
and can also measure heat?

_____

What did the sculpture say to his girlfriend?

_____

What can you find in the very center
of both America and Australia?

_____

What begin your sentences?

_____

What is it that
Kings and queens may cling to power,
and the jesters may have their call,
and the most common but can rule them all?

_____

What kind of illness you may get in China?

_____

What is mine but only you can have?

_____

What would the boy light bulb
say to the girl light bulb?

_____

What is the tallest building in our town?

_____

What is heavy forward but backward is not?

_____

Two women were playing.
They played five games.
Each woman won the same number of games.
How is this possible?

_____

When does Valentine's Day
come after Easter?

_____

What do you call two birds in love?

_____

What can be right, but never be wrong?

_____

What make things short,
but pretty long itself?

_____

What type of weapon for SCI-FI characters?

_____

What do you call round and red
and goes up and down?

_____

How does a vampire call his sweetheart?

_____

Why did the man ask his wife for a map?

_____

Would it hurt much
if you dropped a tomato on your toe?

_____

What can store fire breathing animals?

_____

**What do some people avoid,
some people count and
some people just consume?**

_____


**What object is like a teeth but can't bite?**
1) Comb    2) Toy    3) Smile


**Why is it that nowadays, it's very difficult to
find handsome, sensitive, caring men?**

_____


**How do you spell a pretty girl
with only two letters?**

_____


**How many seconds are there in one year?**

_____


**What will go within you, and destroy you,
but only because you wanted me too?**

_____

What is a seed with three letters in  name,
take away the last two
and I still sounds the same?
1) Tea    2) Pea    3) Bee

What happened when the man realized
he was in love with his backyard?

_____

What did the man with a broken leg
say to his nurse?

_____

What is it that a man can use for shaving,
polishing his shoes, and sleeping in?

_____

What wear a green jacket on the outside,
white jacket as a second layer
and red jacket inside,
and pregnant with a lot of babies?

_____

What kind of dog that chases anything red?

_____

What did the undertaker die of?

_____

What do farmers must give their wives
on Valentine's Day?

_____

Why did Carbon marry Hydrogen?

_____

Why is it impossible to starve in the desert?

_____

What is this precious stone
as clear as diamond,
seek it out while the sun's near the horizon
though you can walk on water with power,
try to keep it,
and it will vanish in an hour?

_____

What have thirteen hearts
but no body or soul.

_____

Do you know a word in the English language
that uses all the vowels including "y"?

_____

What did the Valentine card
say to the stamp?

_____

Can you differentiate
love and marriage?

_____

What is it that you can cut with a knife
and never see a mark?

_____

What do you use
between your head and your toes,
and the more you work, the thinner it grows?

_____

**What shoot but never kills.**
1) Gun    2) Camera    3) Telescope

**What is something that shines
up in the sky at night,
and changes to rodents that gnaw and bite?**

_____

**What do you call the three rings off marriage?**

_____

**What did the man say
about his Korean girlfriend?**

_____

**If there were nine birds sitting on a
bench and a hunter shot one of them,
how many would be left?**

_____

**What is this two in a corner, 1 in a room,
0 in a house but 1 in a shelter?**

_____

Who roam through the lands
hoping to rescue his love.
He search high and low, and will stamp on
you if you get in his way!

_____

If it takes three minutes to steam a hotdog,
how long will it take to steam three hotdogs?

_____

What did the man squirrel say
to the woman squirrel on Valentine's Day?

_____

Why did the cannibal break up
with his girlfriend?

_____

What will you do to make seven
an even number?

_____

What is it that you can build or destroy
and let creativity soar but be careful at night?

_____

**What increase head turning rate**
**tremendously for women at beaches?**

_____

**What do you mean by "bacteria"?**

_____

**What game can be dangerous**
**and not good to your mental health?**

_____

**What  object goes up and down**
**but doesn't move?**

_____

**What is a ring that is square?**
1) Boxing Ring
2) Wedding Ring
3) Cheese Ring

**What is a living
following wealthy and beautiful?**

_____

**What is it that comes down, but never goes up?**

_____

**What does Santa Claus use when he goes skiing?**

_____

**Why is it that basketball players love donuts?**

_____

**Can you measure feet  in a yard?**

_____

**What can you find on body builders
or in the drink aisle?**

_____

What stink up your breath
and fights evil vampires?
1) Onion    2) Garlic    3) Oil


What object do Martians eat for breakfast?

_____


What do you think
a Cheerleader's favorite food?

_____


Who won if two silk worms were in a race?

_____


Who is this person
who pretends to be someone else?

_____

What is this kind of object that
you write on  and secrets keep,
in places never seen,
spin like a top,
though stiff as a board,
and often described like a mop?

_____

Can you differentiate
a dog and a basketball player?

_____

Why is it that  golfer wear two pairs of pants?

_____

Why is it that cows have bells?

_____

What is a house with  two occupants,
sometimes one, rarely three,
break the walls,
eat the boarders, then throw away me?

_____

What is the kind of ant that's good at Math?

_____

Does a man living in New York
be buried in California?

_____

How do football players
stay cool during a game?

_____

What do you call a sheep that practices karate?

_____

What occurs once in a second,
once in a month, once in a century,
yet not at all in an hour,
or a week or a year?

_____

What is the noblest musical instrument?

_____

What is black within and red without,
with four corners round about?

_____


What do you  think is the hardest part
about skydiving?

_____


What time is it when you can't read a clock?

_____


What did one light bulb say
to another light bulb?

_____


What object is it that
every night, told what to do,
and each morning will do what you told.
but still don't escape your scold?

_____

What has seen in the water.
and seen in the sky,
and even  in the rainbow?
1) Blue     2) Green     3) Red


What two days of the week
start with the letter "T"?

_____


Why is it that the basketball player
in trouble with the bank?

_____


Where does a player who weighs 175
kilograms sit on a bus?

_____


What makes you weak
at the worst of all times,
keeps you safe and fine,
makes your hands sweat ,
and your heart grows cold,
it visits the weak, but seldom the bold?

_____

What is this glittering points
that downward thrust,
sparkling spears that never rust?

_____

Why is it that A likes a flower?

_____

What can you get when you
vampire and teacher?

_____

What room do tadpoles change?

_____

Why is it that the farmer did not cry
when his dairy cow fell off the cliff?

_____

What does a young man wants to have,
but when he has it he no longer wants it,
blade in hand he attacks it,
and does his best to remove it,
yet he knows that it is all in vain?

_____

What do you call a yellow fork
from tables in the sky,
by inadvertent dropped the awful cutlery
of mansions never quite disclosed,
and never quite concealed
the apparatus of the dark
to ignorance revealed?

_____


Why is it that the letter "A" likes noon?

_____


Where do cows go to dance?

_____


What do pandas have that other animals lack?

_____


How do porcupines kiss each other?

_____


What can be hairy and itchy all over,
hang on a stick,
and can be the scariest thing you have ever seen
that can stand in the middle of nowhere?

_____

What is a single syllable that is claim,
black was the most famous name;
fetal to mortals here below,
thousands have slain in a single blow?

———————————

What do you call "a fly" that has no wings?

———————————

What is this kind of cup doesn't hold water?

———————————

What type of dress that can never be worn?

———————————

Which is faster, heat or cold?

———————————

What is it that the voice is tender
and waist is slender,
and often invited to play,
yet wherever you go,
it must take a bow
or else it has nothing to say?

———————————

Why do we call our own language
their mother tongue?

_____


What do you keep doing
to avoid lens dryness?

_____


Who will fix your mistakes,
although far from the point?

_____


What do you mean by minimum?

_____


What can be entertaining until you realize
some pieces have been lost?

_____

What sits in a corner
while travelling abroad?

_____

What letter can do the work in one day
that you can also do in two days?

_____

What goes inside the boots
and outside the shoes?

_____

What is this that without coolant,
you'll have some trouble?

_____

What is it that got a wave but no sea?

_____

What kind of coat
that can only be put on when wet?

_____

*Page 1:* Nail Polish / She wanted to see the waterfall. / You can jump out of the lowest step. /slow pygmies / He wanted to have a hot time. / Loud

*Page 2:* Lint / Baldness / Lawsuit / "Are you sleeping?"/ Student: Obviously it is the past tense. / Sibling

*Page 3:* Future / Husband and wife / Tan Coat / It's the same for both stated seasons (24 hours). / Funny Bunny / Pattern

*Page 4:* Joke / To a horsepital. / Woman / Mooosical Chairs / He wanted to save time. / Age

*Page 5:* Last Name / "The Q." (queue) / Looking at yourself in a mirror. / Boxer / He wanted to see time fly. / Air

*Page 6:* Fingernails / Ohio / Because of her crash diet. / Stranger / She wanted to have sweet dreams. / Dictionary

*Page 7:* Lead / When he is short of money. / Destiny / Shall we go for a dip?/ Pushing yourself away from the table. / Knowledge

*Page 8:* Compass / The letter n. / The captain was standing on the deck / Carlos (It's pronounced "carless") / Coffin

*Page 9:* Earth / An unidentified crying object! / Pay the bull. / Week / The license plate number of the vehicle that hit you. / Wholesome

*Page 10.* Lounger / The No-bell prize! / Twelve months / Begins / A river. / Marriage

*Page 11:* Ruler / None! None of them have "c", "o", "m" or "n" in them. / The roll was not good enough. / Love / Baby tigers./ Binary

*Page 12:* Human / Because seven eight nine (seven ate nine) / Roots / Automobile. / Rubber band - because it stretches. / Arrow

**Page 13:** Teeth / "Wrong" / Poison / Submarine / Running out of petrol! / Tea Bag

**Page 14:** Secret / C-A-T / Balance / Clever / Ice cream, cheese...and three cows. / Money

**Page 15:** Death / Fry-day! / Drum / Microwave / When there's a change in the weather! / Elevator

**Page 16:** Temper / "The C" (The sea) / Fist / Snow / A hole / Voice

**Page 17:** Rain / Loud crowd / Socks / Mask / Your aUnts, Uncles, and coUsins. (They all need U.) / Newspaper

**Page 18:** Bed / They are Saturday and Sunday. All the others are weak (week) days. / Bird's shadow / Dragon / The one with the biggest head. / Shoe

**Page 19:** Coffee / Because it's too far to walk. / Stage / Grass / A screwdriver! / Your word

**Page 20:** Road / Because he/she was going to high school! / Bananas / Slipper / N, R, G (energy) / Wedding Ring

**Page 21:** Odometer / The roof / Jail / Toothpick / Normal / Heart

**Page 22:** Tissue / Tomorrow / Sunshine / Anthem / Hold it and then let it go. / Bullet

**Page 23:** Particles / The letter N / Teenager / To keep his pants up. / Reflection

**Page 24:** Friendship / "i" (I) / Bees / Air Force / Ex-pla-nation / Clone

**Page 25:** Thoughts / A sandwich / Silk / Guilty / Glad dad / Smoke

**Page 26:** Electricity / None. A hole is empty. / Rock / Bicycle / There is a fan in every seat. / Music

**Page 27**: Shadow / All of them / Saddle / Forgiveness / Why bother, he won't come anyway. / Memory

**Page 28:** Red Blood Cell / A tennis ball / Spark / Alcohol / Because it wanted to do some eggsploring! / Time

**Page 29:** Ticket / A horse and its rider. / Pep Talk / Tarzan / Water / Gravity

**Page 30:** Dream / leap-peal / Letter / The Empire State Building can't jump! / Scale

**Page 31:** Priest / A squirrel / Five minutes / "y" (Why?") / I Love You

**Page 32:** Atlas / Eight / Sugarcane / Rubik's Cube / Run faster than anyone else. / Oasis

**Page 33:** Baseball / Your lap. (good for phrasal 'stand up', and 'laptop', lap-dog, etc.) / Salad / Eyelashes / He didn't have anybody to take. (any BODY) / Shave

**Page 34:** Lint / B / Evergreen / Magnet / Dam! / Purr

**Page 35**: Hiss / One thousand / Chessmen / Fire / Century

**Page 36:** Pixel / Because it's too far to walk there. / Skeleton / Ring / One's roaring with pain the other's pouring with rain / Atlantic

**Page 37**: Drama / The letter R , because it makes a cow into a crow! / Portrait / Quick Draw / Gorilla

**Page 38:** Bungee / Europe - You see you're up / Train / Emerald / Your right elbow. / Copycat

**Page 39:** GPS / Only one-the last one! / Doorknob / Military Time / Smiles, because there is a mile between the first and last s. / Delete

***Page 40:*** Case / U / Cornfield / Bumblebee / A bottle / Touchdown

***Page 41:*** Kilt / Expennsylvania / Octopus / Stockings / I didn't even know sheep could knit! / Belt

***Page 42:*** Valley / It loses its cool. / You will light the match stick first. / Rootbeer / Wet ones. / Hunger

***Page 43:*** Wine / goat-toga / Elvis Parsley / Celery (Salary) / A jeweler sells watches. A jailer watches cells. / Wig

***Page 44:*** Justice / When you're a mouse! / Party / Honeydew / Neither. A rooster can't lay eggs / History

***Page 45:*** Kiss / Sweet Corn / Cork / Student -The sausage! / Baking Soda

***Page 46:*** Sword / Color-ado / Zucchini (zoo-cchini) / Jam / Quickly! / Log

***Page 47:*** Imagination / Your temperature. / Ice Cream / Gum / Because they always carry their combs! / Pride

***Page 48:*** Fart / The cold shoulder. / Papaya / Mushroom / A telephone / Horizon

***Page 49:*** Hyphen / Your fingernail! / Cookie / Recess pieces / There is no smoke from an electric train. / Hearse

***Page 50:*** Pineapple / The capital of "England" is E / School / We're getting too old for this. / John who suddenly woke up, said, "Who, me?" / Cherry

***Page 51:*** Sonnet / Comedihens! / If you are a teenager / Orientation / Getting older. / Ten

***Page 52:*** Billiard Table / Footsteps / Because they never let you finish a sentence. / A mitten./ A garbage truck / Boat

**Page 53:** L / Their mother was in the pen and they did not know how long her sentence would be. / The truth / Periodic / No idea. (No eye deer) / Tow Truck

**Page 54:** Busboy/ Pretty kitty / Spam / Bridge / Wild child / Calculator

**Page 55:** Bully / Rare chair / Assorted Nuts / Fish-hook/ It wasn't raining. / Joggling

**Page 56:** Scratch / Peerless / Yam / Nine / Termite

**Page 57:** Bumper Car / Mad lad / Rust / Let me atom / Shy fly / Burp

**Page 58:** Home Run / Twenty. You counted the same horses coming and going. / Carbon / Barium / Neither. They're both bad! / Lungs

**Page 59:** Audience / Mercury / I love you with all my art. / The letter R / Capital

**Page 60:** Aces / Kung-flu! / My heart / I love you a whole watt / The library. (It has the most stories.)

**Page 61:** Ton / They played different people. / When you are looking in the dictionary / Tweet hearts / An angle. / Abbreviation

**Page 62:** Laser / A tomato in a lift! / His ghoul-friend / He got lost in her eyes / Yes, if it were in a can. / Dungeon

**Page 63:** Calories / A Comb / They already have boyfriends / QT. / Twelve. January second, February second, March second… / Drugs

**Page 64:** Pea / He wed his plants / I have a crutch on you. / A razor, a brush, and a pair of pajamas. / Wa-termelon

*Page 65:* Bulldog / Coughin' (coffin) / Hogs and Kisses / The bonded so well / Because of all the sandwiches (sand which is there) / Ice

*Page 66:* Deck of Cards / Unquestionablely! / Stick with me, we'll go places / Love is a sweet dream, marriage is the alarm clock / Water / Soap

*Page 67:* Camera / star-rats / The engagement ring, the wedding ring and the suffering / She was his Seoul mate. / None. The noise of the gun would frighten the others away. / R

*Page 68:* Mario / Three minutes, if they're in the same pot. / I am nuts about you. / She was not his taste. / Take off the s. / Minecraft

*Page 69:* Bikini / The back entrance of a cafeteria. / Marbles because you might lose them. / A staircase. / Wedding Ring

*Page 70:* Paparazzi / Rain / The North Pole / Because they can dunk them. / It depends on how many people are standing in it. / Six Pack

*Page 71:* Garlic / Unidentified frying objects. / Cheerios / Neither, it ended in a tie / Impostor

*Page 72:* Floppy Disk / One drools, the other dribbles / Just in case he got a hole in one. / Because their horns don't work. / Peanut

*Page 73:* Accountant / No! He's still living! / They stand next to the fans. / Lamb chop / The letter N / Upright Piano

*Page 74:* Chimney / The ground / Time to get glasses / You are the light of my life. / Alarm-Clock

*Page 75:* Blue / Tuesday and Thursday? NO, today and tomorrow! / He kept bouncing checks / Wherever he wants to. / Fear

*Page 76:* Icicles / Because the B (Bee) is after it. / Blood Test / Croak room / There's no use crying over split milk. / Beard

*Page 77:* Lightning / Because it's in the middle of the dAy. / Meatball . / Baby Panda / Very carefully. / Scarecrow

*Page 78:* Plague / You call it "a walk" / Cupcake / Address / Heat, because you can catch a cold. / Violin

*Page 79:* Because our father seldom get a chance to use it. / Blink / Eraser / A very small mother! (minimom) / Puzzle

*Page 80:* Stamp / W (Double u- Double you) / Ankles / Radiator / My hair / Paint

# CONCLUSION

Thank you again for buying this book! I hope you enjoyed with my book. Finally, if you like this book, please take the time to share your thoughts and post a review on Amazon. It'd be greatly appreciated! Thank you!

Next Steps
– Write me an honest review about the book –
I truly value your opinion and thoughts and I will incorporate them into my next book, which is already underway.

WWW.THEBOOKHIVE.NET
VISIT PAGE: FACEBOOK.COM/THEBOOKHIVEDOTNET

FOLLOW ME: AMAZON.COM/AUTHOR/MELISSAS

47448417R00050

Made in the USA
Lexington, KY
08 August 2019